Dear Parent:
Your child's l   's here!

Every child learns to read in a different way and at his or her own speed. You can help your young reader improve and become more confident by encouraging his or her own interests and abilities. You can also guide your child's spiritual development by reading stories with biblical values and Bible stories, like I Can Read! books published by Zonderkidz. From books your child reads with you to the first books he or she reads alone, there are I Can Read! books for every stage of reading:

SHARED READING
Basic language, word repetition, and whimsical illustrations, ideal for sharing with your emergent reader.

BEGINNING READING
Short sentences, familiar words, and simple concepts for children eager to read on their own.

READING WITH HELP
Engaging stories, longer sentences, and language play for developing readers.

READING ALONE
Complex plots, challenging vocabulary, and high-interest topics for the independent reader.

ADVANCED READING
Short paragraphs, chapters, and exciting themes for the perfect bridge to chapter books.

I Can Read! books have introduced children to the joy of reading since 1957. Featuring award-winning authors and illustrators and a fabulous cast of beloved characters, I Can Read! books set the standard for beginning readers.

A lifetime of discovery begins with the magical words **"I Can Read!"**

Visit www.icanread.com for information on enriching your child's reading experience.
Visit www.zonderkidz.com for more Zonderkidz I Can Read! titles.

RUBY's
Perfect Day

by Susan Hill
pictures by Margie Moore

Lord, everything you have given me is good.
You have made my life secure.
I am very pleased with what you have given me.
I am very happy with what I have received from you.

—Psalms 16:5-6

ZONDERKIDZ

Ruby's Perfect Day

Copyright © 2006, 2010 by Susan Hill
Illustrations © 2006, 2010 by Margie Moore

Requests for information should be addressed to:

Zonderkidz, Grand Rapids, Michigan 49530

Library of Congress Cataloging-in-Publication Data
Long, Susan Hill
     Ruby's perfect day / by Susan Hill ; [illustrations by Margie Moore].
         p.   cm. — (I can read book)
     Summary: When Ruby Racoon wants to share a perfectly sunny day with her
busy woodland friends, she discovers that perfect days can be spent all by yourself.
     ISBN 978-0-310-72024-9 (softcover)
     [1. Solitude—Fiction. 2. Day—Fiction. 3. Friendship—Fiction. 4. Raccoon—
Fiction. 5. Animals—Fiction.] I. Moore, Margie, ill. II. Title.
     PZ7.L8582Ruq 2010
     [E]—dc22   2009033136

All Scripture quotations unless otherwise noted are taken from the *Holy Bible,
New International Reader's Version*®. NIrV®. Copyright © 1995, 1996, 1998 by
International Bible Society. Used by permission of Zondervan. All rights reserved.

Any Internet addresses (websites, blogs, etc.) and telephone numbers printed
in this book are offered as a resource. They are not intended in any way to be or
imply an endorsement by Zondervan, nor does Zondervan vouch for the content
of these sites and numbers for the life of this book.

Zonderkidz is a trademark of Zondervan.

Editor: Mary Hassinger

Printed in China

10 11 12 13 14 15 /SCC/ 22 21 20 19 18 17 16 15 14 13 12 11 10 9 8 7 6 5 4 3 2 1

For Sara
—S. H.

For Jerry
—M. M.

Ruby Raccoon woke up and stretched.

The sun was shining.

The birds were singing.

The air smelled fresh and sweet.

"This is a perfect day," said Ruby.

"A perfect day from God."

Ruby's tummy rumbled.
"It's a perfect day
for a big breakfast!"

Ruby knocked

at the door of Fiona Fox.

"Fiona," said Ruby,

"will you have breakfast with me?"

"I'm sorry, Ruby," said Fiona.

"I'm too busy to have breakfast
with you today."

"That's okay," said Ruby.

11

Ruby walked home and
made a big breakfast.

She ate enough for two

and got a little tummy ache.

After breakfast,

Ruby sat at her table

under the big tree.

"This is a perfect day," said Ruby.

"A perfect day from God."

The sun made a pattern on the table.

"A perfect day

for a game of checkers!"

Just then, Dan Duck waddled by.

"Dan," called Ruby,

"will you play checkers with me?"

16

"I'm sorry, Ruby," said Dan.

"I'm too busy to play checkers."

"That's okay," said Ruby.

Ruby sat at her table and
made a checkerboard of leaves.
It was a pretty checkerboard,
but the wind blew it away.

The sun moved higher in the sky.

Ruby walked to the top of the hill.

"Thank you, God!" praised Ruby.

"This is a perfect day."

An acorn fell to the ground

and rolled away.

"A perfect day

for a roll down the hill!"

21

Ruby saw Bunny Rabbit hopping by.

"Bunny!" shouted Ruby.

"Will you roll down the hill with me?"

"Sorry! Too busy!" Bunny cried.

"Okay," called Ruby.

Ruby rolled down the hill...

and landed with a bump

at the bottom.

Then she walked home

and sat on a stump

in the afternoon sun.

Ruby thought about her day

and all the gifts from God.

She had made a big breakfast.

She had played

a new kind of checkers.

And she had rolled

down the hill—fast!

"Thank you, God," praised Ruby.

"This is a perfect day!"

Ruby saw a worm wiggling in the mud.

"A perfect day

to work in my garden!"

Ruby began to dig.

She dug, and she dug.

She hummed as she dug.

"This is a perfect day," said Ruby.